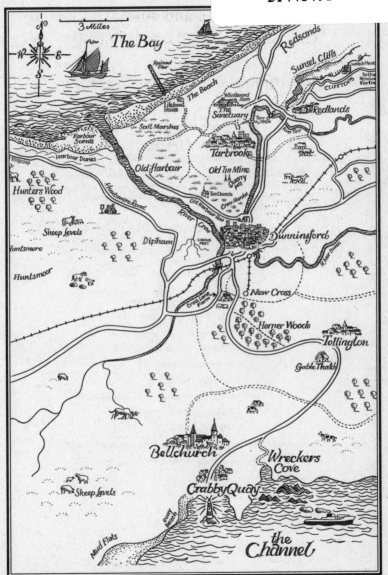

N W E S

3 Miles

The Bay

Redsands

Sunset Cliffs

CLIFFTOPS

to the Roman Fort

Ruined Pier

The Beach

Lifeboat House

Whitsand Farm

The Sanctuary

Redlands

Torr Steps

Salt Marshes

Harbour Sands

River Tarr

Harbour Dunes

Old Harbour

Tarbrooke

Stag's Gap

Hutsmere Road

Old Tin Mine

Quarry Pits

Hunters Wood

Old Harbour Rd

Tin Church

Crow Marsh

River Crow

Sheep Levels

Dipham

Crow's Feet

Dunninsford

River Dunn

Huntsmere

Huntsmoor

Cross Lane Farm

New Cross

Horner Woods

Tollington

Gable Thatch

Bellchurch

Wreckers Cove

Crabby Quay

Mud Flats

the Channel

All the books in this series have been read and approved by the Folly's Farm Sanctuary for Donkeys.

OTHER BOOKS IN THE SERIES

Donkey Disaster
Donkey Drama

Tim Bentley stopped fixing the chain on his mountain bike and looked up at the sound of galloping hoofs and whirring wheels. He knew exactly what was coming. But it was always a spectacle worth watching. Checking his watch, Tim grinned to himself; 'Nine thirty, dead on time.'

Then, just as he expected, bursting into view across Brooke Bridge, thundered Danni Lester and her black racing donkey, Shadow.

'You're late!' Tim yelled, teasing her by tapping his wristwatch. The painted fish-cart was empty and bounced lightly across the grey cobbles, its wheels barely touching the stones.

'No I'm not,' laughed Danni from the driving seat. 'It's exactly nine thirty-one.'

Yellow sparks flashed on the cobbles from Shadow's hoofs as she flicked the reins and took the corner of Tim's cottage at about two hundred miles per hour.

1

Tim laughed as the back of the fish-cart disappeared in a cloud of dust towards the village.

Twenty minutes later she was back with a full load of supplies. Shadow skidded to a halt outside Tim's front gate. The little black donkey stood pawing the ground eager to get going again. The grocery run from Tarbrooke back to The Sanctuary was the highlight of Shadow's week.

Holding the reins taut, Danni leaned from the cart. 'See you in about half an hour,' she grinned, 'unless you fancy a race?'

'No chance,' laughed Tim. 'Nothing could catch that donkey. It's mental.'

'See ya, then,' said Danni. She flicked the reins and called back into the wind, her long dark hair blowing freely behind her. 'Half an hour. Don't be late,' she yelled. 'And I hope you've thought of something!' Then she was gone, aiming the black dynamo back to Whistlewind Farm and her parents' donkey sanctuary.

The Sanctuary—Whistlewind Farm

Kristie Blythe was seventeen and bonkers about donkeys. She worked with Danni's parents, Jenny and Peter Lester, at their donkey sanctuary in Tarbrooke.

She'd been there since the beginning. Five months ago Whistlewind Farm was bought for a song at auction, and became the Lesters' lifelong dream—a donkey retreat, devoted to providing loving care to rescued and unwanted donkeys.

Kristie ran a hand through her mane of fiery copper hair. She was painstakingly planting out a garlic border in the donkeys' vegetable garden when she spotted Tim cycling hell for leather up the long farmyard drive.

'I've got it!' he yelled excitedly. 'I've thought of a fantastic money-making idea to raise funds for the wintering barns. It's brilliant!'

'Brilliant?' exclaimed Danni. She appeared like magic from one of the outbuildings and leapt right into his path. She caught Tim's bike and grabbed his handlebars, standing there with the front wheel clamped between her knees. 'Come on then, Einstein,' she grinned. 'Tell me about this absolutely brilliant idea of yours.'

'It's simple,' began Tim. 'A sponsored point-to-point donkey trek.'

'Point-to-point!' quizzed Danni. 'Which point to what point?'

'The Old Harbour,' said Tim. 'Then cross-country to the south coast and . . .'

' . . . And the lighthouse at Crabby Quay,' guessed Danni. 'Crabby Quay, Bellchurch.'

'Exactly!'

'It sounds perfect,' smiled Kristie, ambling over from the garden. 'A long way, mind you—north coast to south. But perfect for a sponsored trek.'

'How many donkeys shall we take?' asked Danni, getting excited at the idea.

'Only one,' grinned Tim. 'That's the best bit. We just sponsor one donkey—Shadow.'

'Shadow!' laughed Kristie. 'In that case you'll cover the distance in one afternoon. That donkey only has two speeds—stop and manic gallop!'

'I love this idea,' grinned Danni.

Saturday morning. One week later—
the Old Harbour, Tarbrooke

The point-to-point donkey trek idea had turned out to be an instant success with everyone. Both Jenny and Peter Lester thought it was brilliant. And sponsors had been lining up all week, to pledge money towards the building of two much-needed wintering barns for the Sanctuary. The challenge was on. And the little black donkey was eager to get started. He stood, ready in harness.

The plan was that Kristie and Tim would accompany Danni on two other donkeys.

'We'll follow behind with our collection buckets and hand out Sanctuary leaflets,' said Kristie. She let out Jasper's girth strap a notch, as he was belching loudly, and pushed a riding hat down firmly onto her head.

Tim roared with laughter. 'We don't have much choice but to follow behind,' he said, patting Daisy, his own gentle grey. The old donkey was trying to demolish a planter full of marigolds. 'If we're lucky, we might just catch a glimpse of Shadow's fish-cart before Danni disappears with him into the sunset.'

'She'd better not disappear anywhere,' said Kristie. 'I've promised Jenny and Peter that I wouldn't let her out of my sight for one second.'

'We should mount up then,' grinned Tim. 'It looks like they're ready for the off.'

Danni had already settled herself comfortably into the little fish-cart and was waving to a small crowd who had come to see them off.

Shadow was pumping his legs up and down like pistons, ready to run like a woolly whirlwind. Danni flicked the reins and the black donkey shot forward like a bullet from a gun. The fish-cart whizzed along the old harbour road and followed the River Crow towards Dunninsford Town.

Danni shot a quick glance back over her shoulder, and laughed at Tim and Kristie as they struggled to keep up on Daisy and Jasper.

It was forty-five miles to Bellchurch. The route plan was to travel fifteen miles a day, with two overnight stops along the way. Danni's mum had made all the arrangements with friends in New Cross and Tollington. Jenny herself was planning to drive down on the last day, to be there at the lighthouse when Danni and Shadow came thundering into the home stretch along Crabby Quay.

Danni knew that she couldn't just let Shadow run his legs off—even though he would have been more than happy to do so. She decided to give him his head for at least a mile, then pull him up to a more sedate speed, and wait for the others at the Tin Church, halfway to Dunninsford. After all, she didn't want poor Kristie to have a fit. Or wear Daisy and Jasper out before they had even started.

Shadow's bristly black ears pointed forward like lances as he raced along. No one quite knew where the little donkey originally came from. Shadow was the first resident at The Sanctuary (the Lesters liked to refer to the donkeys as residents) and was acquired from a group of travellers who couldn't handle him. The friendly travellers wanted a nice, quiet donkey, and had bought Shadow in haste at a market somewhere in the north of England.

They were more than happy when the Lesters offered him a safe, permanent home. And the Lesters were more than delighted to have him.

Shadow was a dynamo. At first he was a real handful. An absolute nightmare. But now he was the family pet and guard donkey. That was another of Shadow's talents. This little donkey

had the ability to bray at least three times louder than any other, normal donkey. It didn't sound much like normal braying either. More like a fog-horn. It was ear splitting.

The road ahead flashed beneath lightning hoofs and thundering wheels. A contrast to the sleepy River Crow, flowing gently alongside.

In the distance, to the left, Danni could see the derelict towers of the old tin mine silhouetted against the skyline. The sun was baking. It was a real scorcher of a day.

The Tin Church—Crow Marshes

'Whoa!!' yelled Danni into the rush of air. Travelling with Shadow at least keeps you cool, she thought to herself. The wind comes at you, gale force!

She pulled on the reins, and eventually Shadow skidded to a grinding halt outside the small church.

'We've got to work on these brakes of yours, Shad!' The little black donkey flicked back his ears, then threw back his head and brayed. 'Hee Hawww!'

Danni plugged two fingers into her ears and laughed. 'I bet even Kristie and Tim heard that,' she said. And they did!!

Danni took her binoculars and squinted into the sunshine. She looked back along the length of road, then closed one eye as she suddenly remembered that a lens had recently dropped out.

The road was dead straight with no humps.

'Here they come!' she grinned. Shadow swung his head round. Through the binoculars Danni could see Daisy and Jasper ambling along, flat out, at a snail's pace.

'It's a good job they're taking the goods train from Dunninsford,' said Danni, 'or we'll never get to New Cross!'

Shadow couldn't understand a single word that Danni said, but she liked talking to him all the same. She liked the way his long bristly ears twitched like a rabbit's as he listened, picking up every sound.

'I'll give you a nice drink while we're waiting for those two,' said Danni. She leaped from the cart and kicked two wooden brake wedges beneath the rear wheels. Then she took a washing-up bowl from under the seat and poured some water from a big plastic bottle.

Shadow stuck his nose in the bowl and blew bubbles.

'You're supposed to drink it,' said Danni. She ran her hand along the length of his back.

He wasn't even sweating. She gave him a good hard pat, then scratched his chin.

The Tin Church was tiny. It was called the Tin Church because it was made of corrugated tin. The old mining community built it years ago. Now it was a popular tourist site. It also had an outside tap. Danni went to refill the water bottle.

Some holidaymakers were visiting the church and made a huge fuss of Shadow as they came out.

Danni told them all about the good work being done at The Sanctuary and the point-to-point trek to raise funds for the wintering barns. They made a donation to the cause and took Shadow's photograph.

'You can pick up a leaflet from those two slowcoaches,' said Danni, pointing down the road at the approaching escorts. Then she went to refill the water bottle ready for Daisy and Jasper.

'He's a real smasher, isn't he,' said a man with a large plastic container who had also come to use the tap. Danni recognized him from the group she was speaking to earlier.

'Have your friends left you behind?' she joked.

'Oh, I'm not with them,' smiled the visitor politely as he unscrewed the cap off his giant bottle. 'I just stopped off to fill this monster. But I'm glad I did,' he added. 'It was nice to hear all about The Sanctuary and your fund-raising trek.'

At that moment, Shadow called to Danni with a noisy bray. He had suddenly caught Daisy and Jasper's scent on the wind.

'Wow! He's a noisy one,' said the man, pretending to be deafened. 'He could wake the dead with a voice like that!'

Danni laughed. She liked this holidaymaker. He was friendly and funny.

'I've got a mate with a fishing boat called Shadow,' he said, filling his container. 'It's really called *La Sombra*,' he added. 'That's

spanish for "The Shadow". It's painted black too, just like your donkey.' Then he picked up his bottle and said goodbye. 'I hope to see you again. Maybe I'll catch you at Crabby Quay. Bye,' he smiled. And he was gone.

Dunninsford—Midday

There was quite a crowd waiting at the market town of Dunninsford. Shadow hurtled into the main square, bringing the fish-cart to a screeching halt beneath the clock tower.

Suddenly they were completely surrounded by well-wishers. Danni kicked in the brake wedges and beamed a smile at all the people queuing up to meet Shadow and add coins to his collection box.

'What a nice little donkey,' said one person.

'Does he bite?' asked another. 'I once knew a donkey that bit clean through the rails of its paddock. Teeth like a chainsaw.'

Danni laughed. 'No, he doesn't bite. Shadow's as gentle as a lamb.'

Some children petted and stroked the little black donkey. One girl wanted to feed him a juicy carrot.

'Hold it flat on the palm of your hand like this,' demonstrated Danni. Shadow crunched the carrot noisily.

'He's a beauty, isn't he,' remarked a sweet old lady. 'He reminds me of my Blackie, when he was young.' She stroked Shadow's face as she spoke.

'Do you have a donkey?' asked Danni.

Suddenly, the old lady looked sad. 'I've always kept donkeys,' she said. 'Never one, mind you. Always two. It's best if you keep them in pairs, you know. Donkeys are very sociable,' she added. 'They need the company.'

Then tears appeared in the old lady's eyes. 'My Blackie died six months ago,' she said. 'And poor Dixie didn't know what to do with herself. She was his mate. She didn't like being in the field on her own. That's why, the other day, I let the donkey farm take her. Dixie will be better off there. He was a nice man. He'll look after her, and she'll be with other donkeys.'

Danni was about to ask the name of the donkey farm when Shadow suddenly threw up his head and deafened the crowd.

'Hee-Hawwww!' brayed Shadow at the top of his lungs. The little donkey had just spotted his two friends, Daisy and Jasper, entering the square. And when Danni turned round again, the sweet old lady had gone.

Dunninsford Railway Station—
later that afternoon

'I suppose you think this is really funny,' laughed Tim. He was pulling a face at Danni and trying to encourage Daisy up a ramp and into the goods van. It was like pushing an elephant up hill with a rope. 'She won't budge,' complained Tim. Even Kristie was laughing.

'Donkeys can be very stubborn,' she said. 'But if you know how to treat them right, they'll do anything for you.' She turned to Danni and winked. 'Watch this!'

Kristie gave Daisy a kiss on the forehead and rubbed her hairy muzzle. 'Come on, girl,' she cooed. The fat donkey cocked her head, then shot up the ramp after Kristie, without a moment's hesitation, dragging Tim behind her.

'How on earth did you do that?' Tim was gobsmacked. One minute Daisy was glued to the station platform. And the next, she was happily standing inside the goods van, waiting for an easy ride to the next town.

'Easy peasy,' grinned Kristie. She opened her closed fist and revealed her secret weapon —a polo mint. Daisy rumbled a contented snuffle and lipped the bribe from her open palm.

Jasper's nostrils twitched. He had caught the minty scent and clattered up the metal ramp after them.

'I hope you've got a mint ready,' laughed Danni. 'There's nothing worse than a donkey in a mood.'

'Quick, Kristie!' joked Tim. 'Mints!!'

Danni and Shadow watched as the train slowly pulled out of the station. Jasper and Daisy were getting a comfortable ride into New Cross.

The railway line ran adjacent to the road, so Kristie was able to keep an eye on Danni and Shadow—the dynamic duo. This left Danni free to open Shadow to full throttle and race like a rocket to their first stopover.

This donkey could really move. And a donkey racing against a train was something that no one had ever seen before. All the passengers hung out of the windows and cheered as Danni and Shadow flew alongside like the wind. The passengers were very generous and filled Kristie's and Tim's collection buckets almost to the brim, as they walked the length of the train.

High Street—New Cross

Outside New Cross station, a huge painted banner was stretched across the street. It read: 'support The Sanctuary—point-to-point donkey trek'. There was a silhouette of Shadow in full gallop at one end claiming: 'The world's fastest donkey'.

Kristie and Tim stood beneath it with Daisy and Jasper. The two donkeys snoozed in the shade while Kristie and Tim rattled their collection tins and handed out information and leaflets about The Sanctuary.

A line of people had gathered and stood alongside, waiting to see Danni and Shadow come streaking into the High Street.

'Any minute now,' said Kristie to a little girl standing close. 'It's not every day that you see a racing donkey, is it?'

The little girl shook her head in excited anticipation as a cloud of dust appeared at the end of the street. Then, bursting into full view, with the sound of galloping hoofs and whirring wheels, thundered Shadow.

A huge cheer rang out as he raced up the High Street and screeched to a halt beneath The Sanctuary banner.

Danni leapt from the cart. She let Shadow cool down and gave him a good drink. Then she gave his coat a rub down while she chatted to the gathered crowd.

'We beat you!' whispered Tim in her ear. Danni nudged him in the ribs and laughed.

'I should think so. You were taking it easy on a train!' Shadow waggled his ears and blew a rasping snort as if to say: 'But it *was* close, wasn't it?'

Kristie looked after the donkeys while Danni and Tim went in all the shops asking if they could leave handouts and flyers on the service counters.

It was amazing how many people had got to hear of the sponsored donkey trek. But Danni and Tim were disappointed to learn that not many people knew about the actual Sanctuary itself.

'Let's hope these leaflets make a difference,' said Tim, dropping a fresh pile onto a counter. 'After all we *are* the only donkey sanctuary on the north coast.'

An elderly man was in the shop and overheard what Tim had just said. He picked up a leaflet and quickly flipped through it. Then he spoke. 'You're not that farm then? The one that's been offering to take people's old and sick donkeys?'

At first Danni and Tim didn't understand what the man was saying. Then the penny dropped as Danni suddenly remembered her conversation with that sweet old lady back in Dunninsford.

'No, we're not *that* donkey farm,' answered Danni politely. 'We're a retirement home for donkeys called The Sanctuary, just outside Tarbrooke. And until now we thought we *were* the only donkey home in the area. I'd like to know more about this other farm,' she added.

25

'I don't know the name of it,' said the man. 'But I *do* remember the chap saying it was just outside Dipham. That's very near you, isn't it?'

'It's almost on our doorstep,' exclaimed Tim. 'But I've not heard of a donkey farm there, have you, Danni?'

Danni shook her head. 'Never.'

'Well, that's where this donkey farm chap said it was,' insisted the old man. 'He took Charlie Macey's old grey off his hands only yesterday. Said he would put him out to grass in good company. The trouble is, old Charlie misses that donkey already. He wants to go and visit, but he feels daft because he doesn't remember the farm's name.'

'I bet Kristie would know,' said Danni. 'If there *is* a donkey farm in Dipham, then she'll definitely know of it.'

Cross Lane Farm—New Cross

'I don't believe it,' said Kristie. 'That's three people in forty-eight hours who have given their donkeys to some stranger from a donkey farm that no one's heard of!'

She drew up a chair beside Danni and Tim. They were settled in at Cross Lane Farm—the arranged stopover—for the night.

Kristie poured three Cokes. Then she told Danni and Tim about the third donkey owner she had spoken to, that same afternoon in the High Street.

'Two donkeys!' explained Kristie. 'This owner had given two donkeys, Dolly and Captain, to a charming man from this same donkey farm in Dipham. A donkey farm that I don't think exists. I'm almost certain of it!'

'That's three people, four donkeys,' sighed Tim.

'I know,' worried Kristie. 'And I don't like it!'

'I wonder what's happened to them,' said Danni. 'I wonder where those donkeys are?' Her voice snapped Kristie out of her thoughts.

'I dread to think,' answered Kristie. She didn't say any more. She didn't want to upset

Danni and Tim with what she was really thinking.

Later that evening, Kristie telephoned The Sanctuary. She asked the Lesters if they knew of this so-called donkey farm in Dipham. Neither Jenny nor Peter had ever heard of it. But Jenny promised Kristie that she would make it her business to find out.

Cross Lane Farm—the following morning

After the donkeys had been fed their breakfast, Danni decided to give Shadow a proper grooming.

A roving reporter from the local radio station was coming out to the farm. And although Shadow wouldn't be seen by the listeners, Danni wanted him to look his best. It was all good publicity for The Sanctuary.

'Don't mention anything about the Dipham donkey farm,' warned Kristie. Her voice sounded troubled. 'Only talk about the fund-raising trek and all the good work we do at The Sanctuary. We don't want local radio giving people the wrong idea.'

Danni and Tim exchanged a glance. 'What does she mean?' whispered Tim. 'Giving people the wrong idea?'

'I think there's something Kristie's not telling us,' admitted Danni. 'Try and find out what it is while you're on the road to Tollington.'

Kristie and Tim were going on ahead to pave the way while Danni and Shadow stayed back for the radio interview.

It wouldn't take Shadow long to catch up anyway. They would still all arrive together at Tollington, as planned.

Shadow's black woolly coat was all fluffed out after Danni had finished with him. The little donkey's ears waggled with pleasure as Danni combed his bristly mane. She checked his hoofs then fitted his bridle and harnessed him to the fish-cart.

Shadow chewed on his bit and jangled his reins. He knew that when he was in harness, it was time to run. And Shadow was eager to get started.

But first there was the radio interview. Danni checked her wristwatch. It was nine thirty and a mobile broadcasting unit was cruising up the long farmyard drive.

Danni felt butterflies the size of sparrows fluttering inside her tummy. She was about to represent The Sanctuary on local radio and felt a little nervous.

'Just talk about the donkey trek and all the good work that we do at The Sanctuary.' Danni remembered Kristie's advice and suddenly the butterflies didn't seem half as bad. But she still felt nervous.

Cross Lane Farm—10.30a.m.

The interview had gone really well. Danni felt she'd done a good job and was now keen to get going. Shadow was eager to be away too. The little black racing donkey scraped at the gravel path with his front hoof and blew a snort through his nostrils.

'OK, Shad. Let's go and catch up with those two slowcoaches.' She flicked the reins and Shadow shot off in top gear. Megadrive.

The road out of New Cross was quite bumpy so Danni slowed Shadow down to about seventy miles per hour. She didn't fancy being thrown clear of the cart.

'Whoa, boy!' Shadow strained against the reins, but slowed his pace with a disgruntled whicker to a steady trot. His long ears tick-tocked from side to side like a metronome, measuring his pace.

'You can race as fast as you like along the first decent stretch,' promised Danni. But when the first suitable runway loomed, Shadow was suddenly distracted.

The countryside to the left of the road was heavily wooded with rolling hills far beyond. Shadow seemed particularly interested in a cart

track leading off the main road into those woods. A signpost read; Tollington 8 miles. The little donkey stopped in his tracks, then threw up his head with a deafening Hee-Hawww!!

'Do you really *have* to do that?' laughed Danni, plugging her ears in case he did it again.

Shadow looked back over his withers and harrumphed gruffly.

'What is it, Shad?' Danni asked. The donkey was now staring along the cart track and blowing soft whickers into the air. 'Do you want to take the shortcut through the woods?' Danni quickly studied her map. She saw that the track through the woods sliced a long portion off the main road. 'Now that could be a brilliant idea,' grinned Danni. 'It's cross country, but we could cut a huge chunk off the route and re-join the Tollington road ahead of Tim and Kristie. Now that would be *so* funny if we were there first, waiting for them.'

Shadow waggled his long ears before pointing them up the cart track. Then he pulled the fish-cart off the road and followed his ears. Shadow had made up his mind.

'OK, boy. Let's do it!'

Horner Woods

The cart track was an easy run. The cart's spinning wheels threw a carpet of dried leaves behind them as they cut through the woods.

After ten minutes of flat-out galloping, Danni pulled Shadow down to a trot. The woods were growing thicker and denser.

Shadow raised his nose to the air and sniffed at the wind. Suddenly the woods smelt of smoke. Danni could smell it too!

'Someone's got a bonfire going,' she said. There was nothing to be seen, but the wind was blowing a definite smell of smoke from that part of the woods.

'Come on, Shad. Let's go and find out what's burning.'

Danni steered the fish-cart off the track, through a shallow stream, and into the woods. The trees grew very thick in places. Danni tried to drive slowly and very quietly.

The cart-wheels rustled the undergrowth as Danni and Shadow made their way further and deeper into the woods.

Then, just up ahead, where the trees opened out into a clearing, Danni saw something. It was an old cattle-wagon.

A green canvas tarpaulin was thrown across its roof and pegged up at the front on two poles. The canvas made a canopy with the wagon half hidden underneath.

A few metres from the wagon, a small fire burned slowly. Wispy spirals of smoke rose into the air, disappearing up through the branches of the overhanging trees. There was no one around. The makeshift camp seemed deserted.

Shadow let out an excited snort. 'Shhh!!' whispered Danni. She pressed a finger to her lips, just in case there *was* somebody around. She was snooping and didn't want to be caught. There was something about this wagon that wasn't quite right. For a start, it had foreign number plates and looked really out of place, hidden amongst the trees.

Danni steered Shadow behind a thick bush and eyed the wagon suspiciously. There was still no sign of anyone.

Then suddenly, Danni heard someone whistling and her heart leapt. A man appeared from nowhere. He walked out from the trees heading straight towards them.

Danni gasped and held her breath. She prayed that Shadow wouldn't make a noise and give their hiding place away. The little donkey's ears were sticking straight up in the air. And his nostrils were twitch-twitch-twitching.

Please don't bray, thought Danni. Please!

The man walked right past them, just three metres from their hiding place. He continued whistling and walked back the way Danni and Shadow had come. He carried a big plastic container. Danni guessed that he was heading for the stream to fetch some water.

Suddenly Danni recognized him. It was the happy holidaymaker—the man she had spoken to outside the Tin Church at Crow Marshes.

Danni watched him disappear through the trees. When it was safe to come out of hiding, she tethered Shadow to a branch and approached the wagon. Shadow gave a snort and tried to follow. When he realized that he couldn't, the little donkey threw back his head and filled the woods with his own sweet voice.

All of a sudden, there seemed to be donkeys braying everywhere. The woods echoed the sing-song heee-hawww of calling donkeys. The unmistakable sound of donkeys in distress. Danni would recognize that sound anywhere.

At first Danni couldn't tell where it was coming from. But then, to her horror, she realized that it was coming from inside the cattle-wagon.

The constant braying was creating such a din.

I've got to get out of here, thought Danni, before the driver comes back.

The road to Tollington

Danni raced Shadow through the woods and re-joined the main road four miles outside Tollington. It was twelve o'clock.

'Surely the others haven't passed yet!' Danni told herself. She decided to backtrack along the road to meet them.

Danni felt that she just had to tell Kristie and Tim about the donkeys locked up in that cattle-wagon as soon as possible. She had no proof, but something told Danni that these were the donkeys who were supposedly being taken to the mysterious donkey farm in Dipham. The donkeys who were supposed to be settling into their new home, enjoying the start of a happy retirement. *Not* cooped up in a rotten old cattle-wagon heading for goodness knows where!

It made Danni's blood boil. She was bristling with anger over this ruthless man who had tricked the donkeys' owners into parting with their beloved pets.

Shadow must have sensed something too. He charged along with his head low, ears forward. He didn't look up until he caught Daisy and Jasper's scent as they came ambling over the distant brow of the highway.

Kristie and Tim didn't seem at all surprised when Danni told them about her discovery. Tim had already managed to worm Kristie's fears out of her on their journey. Kristie believed that the captive donkeys were probably on their way to an abattoir somewhere, to be slaughtered and sold as horsemeat.

When Danni told her about the foreign number plates on the cattle-wagon, Kristie knew that all her worst fears had come true. The donkeys were being taken across the channel to be killed. And legally, there was nothing anyone could do to stop them.

Danni and Tim made up their minds straight away. They swore they would do everything they could to rescue those poor donkeys. They were going to get them away from that monster and deliver them to the safety of The Sanctuary. But how!

Gable Thatch Guest House—Tollington

They were met at the guest house in Tollington by a small crowd who had heard Danni's interview on the radio. Danni had mentioned the name of the guest house they were using as a stopover. And the locals had come to offer their support and meet Shadow.

The little donkey was full of it, and enjoying all the fuss and attention. He was a right little show off at times.

Kristie sat in her bedroom facing the mirror. She was pinning up her wild mane of hair, ready for a bath. But she barely noticed her own reflection. Her mind was on those poor, wretched donkeys.

Kristie knew they had stumbled across a terrible racket. That man was running a dishonest scam by tricking innocent people into giving him their donkeys, then selling them abroad as horsemeat.

Kristie had already phoned The Sanctuary and spoken to Jenny Lester. Jenny was driving down the next day to be at Crabby Quay when Danni and Shadow crossed the finish line. Jenny told Kristie not to do anything about rescuing the donkeys until she got there.

'If the driver had made a camp in the woods, then hopefully he's not going anywhere just yet.' That's what Jenny had said. And at least we know where to find him, thought Kristie. The last thing we want right now is to make him suspicious and send him into deeper hiding.

Danni and Tim were next door. They were sharing a bedroom. Danni sat on the top bunk dangling her feet in Tim's face.

'What if Mum gets there and he's gone?' worried Danni. 'What will happen to those poor donkeys then?'

'Don't worry,' Tim reassured her. 'Your mum always thinks of something. And anyway, there's not much we *can* do at the moment, is there? We've just got to remember how lucky it was that you and Shadow found the missing donkeys in the first place!'

But Tim's words didn't comfort Danni much.

'We don't even know the wagon's registration number,' she complained. 'I could kick myself for not writing it down when I had the chance. What if he *does* move the donkeys on. What if he *doesn't* catch a ferry or cross the channel for weeks and just travels around collecting more donkeys. We need the number to leave with the port officials in case he gives us the slip. And I'm going to get it.'

'You can't,' said Tim. 'Kristie won't let you. She was told not to do anything. And that includes you, Danni.'

'But she won't know if we don't tell her,' said Danni. 'You'll cover for me, won't you? If I take Shadow, we can be there and back inside an hour!'

'And what am I supposed to tell Kristie if she asks for you?' worried Tim.

'She could easily be in that bath for an hour,' replied Danni. 'But if she *does* ask, just say I've taken Shadow into town to hand out more flyers. It's still early and the high street's just down the hill. Kristie will swallow that. And with a bit of luck, she won't even ask.'

Then, before Tim could argue, Danni was gone, harnessing Shadow and heading back to Horner Woods.

Shadow ran like the wind. He seemed to know that he was on an important mission, and flew along with his hoofs barely touching the ground. The wheels of his fish-cart were steaming as Danni flicked the reins, letting the little donkey know that he could go as fast as he liked. This was Shadow at his best.

Horner Woods—6.30 p.m.

Danni couldn't remember exactly where the cattle-wagon had been parked up. The woods looked different this time because they had come in from the Tollington side.

'I'm sure it was around here, somewhere,' whispered Danni. The cart moved slowly, almost silently, through the undergrowth.

Shadow rumbled a soft snort. He pulled on the reins and wanted to rush forward into the trees. But Danni kept him back. She didn't want to accidentally charge into the clearing where the cattle-wagon was camped.

Then Danni guessed that Shadow probably knew exactly where the spot was. That's why he was pulling on his reins. Danni held her breath and gave the little donkey his head.

But first she prayed that he wouldn't start braying and give the game away. She was planning to sneak up on the vehicle unobserved. Take down the registration number. And get back to Tollington as quickly as possible.

Shadow seemed to understand perfectly. Without making a sound he pulled the cart swiftly to the clearing where they had first seen the cattle-wagon.

At first Danni thought he'd made a mistake. The clearing was empty. But then she saw tyre marks and the charred remains of the campfire. The reality hit Danni with a sickening thud. An ugly knot twisted itself tightly in her stomach as her heart thumped all the way down to her boots. Danni realized that the cattle-wagon had moved on.

Filled with frustration and disappointment, Danni turned the fish-cart and steered Shadow back though the woods.

She checked her watch—six forty-five. Not bad. Hopefully, Kristie was still soaking in the bath.

Tollington Road

Out of the woods and halfway back along the road to Tollington, Danni suddenly stiffened in the driving seat. Up ahead, not more than two hundred metres away, was a vehicle.

The evening sun was low; hugging the road behind the vehicle, Danni couldn't see it very clearly at first. But it was definitely a van or a wagon of some kind.

Danni flicked the reins and Shadow hit superspeed. They tore along the tarmac runway. Whirring wheels drove them nearer, closer to the slow-moving vehicle.

Then Danni gasped. She could see it now as clear as the bristle-brush mane on Shadow's neck. It was the cattle-wagon from the woods. And it was heading south, which meant—the coast!

Danni was near enough to read the number plate. 112996-DD293. She said it aloud, over and over again, trying to memorize it on freeze-frame inside her head. But she didn't trust her memory that much. This was too important. At least with the registration number, the vehicle could be identified if it turned up at any port.

Danni had no choice but to pull over at the side of the road. She fished in her back pocket

for a pencil and scribbled down the number on a scrap of paper. Mission accomplished!

Gable Thatch Guest House—Tollington

Danni couldn't believe how lucky she'd been to come across the cattle-wagon again. Minutes after writing down the number, it disappeared off the road altogether. She didn't catch sight of it again. But she was really pleased that she could now pass on the number to the port authorities.

Tim looked anxious. He'd been on tenter-hooks for the last hour.

'Well?' asked Danni.

'She hasn't even surfaced,' breathed Tim with relief. Kristie was still in the bathroom drying and taming her wild, frizzy hair into a wild, frizzy style.

'Help me with Shadow,' said Danni. 'Then I'll tell you what happened.'

Outside in the open barn, Tim gave Shadow a good rub down while Danni checked his legs and picked out his hoofs. Then she filled all the donkey's feed buckets and water pails before telling Tim everything.

Daisy and Jasper listened carefully too! Their ears always waggled excitedly at the sound of human voices. Shadow closed his eyes and munched on his barley straw as Danni and Tim gave each donkey a cuddle before going inside for their own supper.

Seated around the dining table, Danni waited for an opportunity to tell Kristie about her trip back to Horner Woods. She knew she was heading for a right telling off. But it had to be done. For the donkeys' sake.

Talk quickly turned to the plight of the captive donkeys, held in the cattle-wagon.

'It's really awful,' said Kristie. 'But at least we now know where they are!'

Danni shot a glance at Tim and sighed. She hadn't found a way yet to tell Kristie that the cattle-wagon had gone.

'Your mum's coming down early tomorrow,' continued Kristie. 'And she's bringing two friends with her. Martin Green from the RSPCA and Robert Richards, a photographer from the *Gazette*. They're planning to confront that con-man in the woods. Catch him by surprise and read him the riot act. Then they'll take charge of the donkeys. He'll have no choice but to hand them over. Martin Green will see to that!' She drew a long breath. 'Then we'll get the donkeys back to The Sanctuary as quickly as possible.'

It all seemed so perfectly planned. But it wasn't going to work. Danni handed a folded piece of paper to Kristie. Then she gulped down a breath. And confessed.

Kristie didn't exactly blow her top. She wasn't pleased either.

'OK. It's a bonus that we now have the vehicle registration number. But I don't know what I'm going to tell Jenny,' worried Kristie. She blew a flyaway corkscrew strand of hair out of her eyes. 'I've got to phone now and tell her that the cattle-wagon's moved on. She's bound to ask how I know. And how I've suddenly got the vehicle's number!'

'Can't we just say that we saw it passing through Tollington,' suggested Tim. He was really good with ideas. 'After all,' he added, 'it *was* heading this way!'

'He's right,' Danni butted in. 'We could easily have seen it if it went through the town!'

'I suppose so,' admitted Kristie. But she warned, 'Don't you *ever* do anything like that again!' Then she finished her supper and went to phone Jenny Lester again.

Danni and Tim checked on the donkeys, settled them down for the night and went to their room. Kristie came in and told them that Jenny and her friends were still coming as planned. Jenny wanted to see Danni and Shadow cross the finish line at Crabby Quay. But first she was going to visit the port and speak to the harbour master. She couldn't notify the police because legally, the louse of a donkey thief hadn't really broken the law. He hadn't actually stolen the donkeys. They'd been *given* to him.

Later that evening

Danni and Tim lay in their bunks. Danni was dead tired, but she couldn't sleep. It was fun at first, lying in the dark, talking with Tim. But then he drifted off to sleep and Danni was left listening to the muffled noises of the guest house.

She lay staring up at the ceiling, waiting for her eyes to get tired. Then she realized that she needed to use the bathroom.

The bunk creaked as Danni sat up and swung her legs out. Tim didn't stir. She opened the bedroom door a crack and peered out.

The bathroom was opposite. She crossed the landing quickly. Re-crossing minutes later, she was about to go back into her room when someone came up the stairs.

It was Mary Giles, landlady of Gable Thatch. She was coming up the stairs, showing an overnight guest to his room. Danni gasped, hardly able to believe her eyes. The overnight guest was the driver of the cattle-wagon. The man who was holding the donkeys.

'Wake up!' Danni dived back into the room and threw herself at Tim. She dragged him off the bunk.

'You'll never guess who's just booked in. And sleeping just down the corridor!'

'Whaaa!!' blinked Tim, still half asleep.

'It's him,' insisted Danni. 'The con-man. He's staying here at the guest house, and sleeping down the corridor.'

Tim was wide awake, now. 'Are you sure?' he asked.

'Positive!' replied Danni. 'Come on. Let's tell Kristie.'

Kristie was outside, doing one last check on the donkeys before going to bed herself. She couldn't believe it when Danni and Tim told her the latest.

There was no sign of the cattle-wagon, though. Kristie went looking but guessed that it

was probably well hidden somewhere, out of sight. It would have been impossible to find it in the dark.

'I bet he's fed up with sleeping rough,' guessed Kristie, 'and fancied a decent bed for the night. He's probably planning to catch the midday ferry tomorrow,' she added.

'Well I hope he is,' smiled Danni. 'Because we're going to be ready for him!'

Kristie sent Danni and Tim back off to bed. She was eager to phone The Sanctuary again to give Jenny Lester the news.

Gable Thatch—the following morning

Danni woke early. Really early. Then she woke Tim with a tooth-rattling shake.

'I couldn't sleep either,' said Danni.

Tim gave her a funny look through bleary eyes. He could easily have slept on for a week.

'I want to be the first down to breakfast,' announced Danni. 'I want to be there when that horrible man comes down. And when he leaves we're going to follow him, and find out where he's hiding those donkeys.'

'Then what?' questioned Tim. 'What can we do except watch him drive them away!'

'We let down his tyres,' grinned Danni. 'Just to make certain that this time he doesn't go anywhere. Then we wait for Mum!'

'I bet she drives down even earlier now that she knows he's here,' said Tim.

But Danni's masterplan was very short lived. No sooner had she gone outside to feed the donkeys their breakfast, when they were met with an unexpected horror. Shadow, Jasper, and Daisy had gone.

Danni's stomach did a triple somersault and landed in her throat like a lump of turnip.

Suddenly she felt sick. Danni and Tim both stood with their mouths hanging open in disbelief, staring into the empty barn where the donkeys should have been.

All that remained was the fish-cart parked in the corner. Danni and Tim were frozen to the

spot. Neither of them could move. Their legs seemed to have died.

Then suddenly, a familiar noise snapped them out of their trance. It sounded far away but it was the unmistakable sound of Shadow, braying at the top of his lungs. And it seemed to be getting closer and closer by the second.

Danni and Tim ran out of the barn. They quickly scanned the road, both up and down, anxiously waiting to see which direction Shadow would be coming from. He was making a terrible racket.

Then they heard the clatter of hoofs against the hard tarmac and shot a glance to the left. Galloping into view along the road raced the little black donkey. A rope attached to his headcollar flew out behind him like an angry snake.

Shadow skidded to a screeching halt, inches from where Danni and Tim stood. 'Hee Hawww!!!'

At the same moment a window at the guest house opened and Kristie's face appeared.

'What on earth's going on?' she demanded. 'Why have you got Shadow out so early? You'll wake the whole house!'

Danni blurted out the whole story as quickly as possible. Kristie shot back inside. Less than a minute later she flew out of the back door, fully dressed.

It was all too obvious what had happened. No way could the donkeys have worked their tethers free. Kristie had doubled-checked them herself before going to bed—No . . . The donkeys had been taken . . . Stolen! It would have been easy. Daisy and Jasper were so docile. And Shadow would do anything for a peppermint.

Luckily, the little donkey had obviously escaped and broken free. As well as being fast, Shadow could be quite feisty when he wanted. Good old Shadow.

'I bet it's him!' accused Danni. 'I bet it's that horrible man. He's added Daisy and Jasper to his collection.'

'And he nearly got Shadow!' added Tim.

'We don't know for sure,' reasoned Kristie, 'but if he is guilty then it's given us a good reason now to involve the police.'

'Let's bash his door down and question him,' said Danni.

'*You* stay here,' ordered Kritsie. 'I'll wake Mary Giles and we'll go and see what he's got to say for himself.'

'Well, he's not likely to own up to anything, is he?' mumbled Tim sarcastically. 'If he thinks he's got away with it, he won't say a word.'

But it was worse than that! When they knocked, no one answered. And when Mary Giles unlocked the door there was no one there. The room was empty. The man had gone.

'That proves it,' said Danni. 'It *was* him. Just like a lousy thief, he's sneaked off in the early hours. And he's taken our donkeys.'

Later that morning

Jenny Lester went absolutely ballistic when she arrived. Then she calmed down and telephoned the police. The police in turn notified the ferry port and set up road blocks. When the cattle-wagon turned up, the driver would be arrested on the spot.

'But what if it doesn't turn up?' asked Danni.

'Then the police will track it down,' said Martin Green, the RSPCA officer.

'It was lucky that you both noted the wagon's number plate when it passed through Tollington,' added Robert Richards, the photographer. 'Otherwise there would be no way the police could ever find it!'

There was a quick exchange of hurried glances between Danni, Tim, and Kristie. Then Jenny continued, 'Don't worry. He won't get away. I'll see to that!'

They all sat down to breakfast, but only Martin and Robert ate anything. Nobody else had much of an appetite. All they could think about was Daisy, Jasper, and all those other poor donkeys locked away in that horrible cattle-wagon.

The outskirts of Bellchurch

Danni and Shadow were back on the road. Her mum had told her that it was still important to finish the sponsored trek.

Danni's radio broadcast had brought in even more willing sponsors. Apparently, The Sanctuary had been inundated with telephone calls. Danni was pleased about that. And now, their planned arrival at Crabby Quay was turning into a local media event.

There were going to be television cameras and everything. It was really great publicity for the cause.

But as Danni and Shadow raced along, all kinds of thoughts were dancing through her mind. She couldn't help wondering if the radio interview had given that horrible man the idea to steal The Sanctuary donkeys. After all, she had told the interviewer all about Daisy and Jasper. And mentioned their stopovers when she was talking about the route. He *knew* they were going to be staying at the guest house. He must have deliberately planned to slip in and out, and steal their donkeys.

I bet he was even thinking of ways to steal Shadow when I first met him outside the Tin Church, she thought.

Shadow tore up the strip of tarmac as he thundered along heading for the southern coastline. His ears pointed forward aiming the cart towards the sea.

Tim, Kristie, Jenny Lester, Martin, and Robert had gone ahead with the horsebox as planned. They wanted to set up the finish line and promote more publicity for The Sanctuary.

Then they were hoping to bring the rescued donkeys safely home, as soon as the police had found and arrested the thief.

Danni should have been thinking of those joint goals. Of crossing the finish line and bringing the rescued donkeys home to The Sanctuary. But her mind was wrestling with other thoughts. It was something that the con-man had said to her when they first met. It troubled Danni because she somehow knew it was important. Only, try as she did, Danni couldn't remember what it was. She ran everything about that first meeting over and over in her head. Frame by frame. It was painful.

Crabby Quay—Bellchurch

The entire quayside was buzzing with people: donkey-lovers and new friends of The

Sanctuary who had come to support the fund-raising event. They crowded the cobbled pavements. A line of coloured flags was strung across the quay between two lampposts. The finish line—a thin red tape—was pulled taut beneath it.

Jenny Lester stood with Tim and Kristie while Robert took photographs. They had been in contact with the police and the harbour master at the ferry port. But so far, no one had tried to book a foreign cattle-wagon for a crossing. And the road blocks had nothing to report.

Overhead, the sun was a white fuzzy ball. Hot and bright. Blinking, Tim turned to Jenny and asked, 'What if he doesn't bother to take a ferry? What if he finds another way to get the donkeys across the channel?'

Approaching the junction into Bellchurch

At exactly that same moment, Danni remembered what the con-man had told her. His words hit her like a hammer. Hard.

La Sombra, the Spanish word for Shadow. It was the name of his friend's fishing boat.

Suddenly everything slotted into place. And Danni felt sick.

The cattle-wagon had foreign number plates. And now there was a definite connection with a foreign fishing boat.

Those poor donkeys weren't leaving from any ferry port, Danni realized. They were being sneaked out of the country on a rotten old fishing smack. *La Sombra* would chug into some bay, unnoticed, claim its cargo, then disappear across the channel without a trace. And no one would be any the wiser or have the slightest clue to their whereabouts. The donkeys were doomed.

It made Danni so cross thinking about it. She was dizzy with anger. The road ahead sloped down towards the coast. Danni and Shadow could see Bellchurch quite clearly. It was only two miles away now, with Crabby Quay and the lighthouse rising below in the distance.

Danni pulled Shadow up to a slower pace. She didn't want to arrive at the Quay with him blowing and working a sweat. Shadow wouldn't have minded though. The little donkey could run forever. And would be very happy to prove it given half the chance.

The wheels of the fish-cart stopped whirring and spitting up hot dust as Danni cut Shadow's speed by half. The countryside around her became less of a blur as they slowed to approach a junction in the road. They stopped at a signpost. It offered two directions.

Directly ahead, sticking to the main road, lay Bellchurch and Crabby Quay. And beyond this, glinting blue-grey under the sun, lay the shimmering sea.

The left fork offered a winding route down to Wreckers' Cove.

Danni shielded her eyes against the sun and peered towards the horizon. She could make out the long, low shape of a small ship or boat.

'I bet that's the ferry,' she told herself. But somehow it looked the wrong shape.

Shadow took advantage of the stop and snatched at a bunch of dandelions growing at the roadside. Danni reached for the binoculars. She focused on the vessel. It wasn't the ferry at all. It looked more like a fishing smack.

The fine hairs on the back of Danni's neck stood on end as she realized what she was looking at. It was *La Sombra*. A fishing boat that could slip in and out of a wreckers' bay like a shadow!

Dropping the binoculars into the back of the cart Danni took up the reins and made her choice—Wreckers' Cove. She just *had* to find out if the cattle-wagon was there, waiting for *La Sombra* to come in.

Wreckers' Cove

The winding road down to the cove grew steeper and narrower. Suddenly it was no more than a lane, snaking its way between grassy hedgerows, sloping down towards a pebble beach.

Danni could hardly see a thing up ahead. Most of the cove was hidden from view by a final twist in the lane. Steep cliffs, which flanked the entrance to the beach also blocked most of her view.

But what she *could* see was the distant strip of sparkling sea. And a fishing boat, chugging its way through the water, getting nearer and nearer.

Danni pulled up the cart, kicked in the brake blocks, and left Shadow to crop the bank while she crept down to the beach.

The cove slowly opened up before her. But the shingle ridge and the pebble beach beyond was deserted.

Perhaps I've been letting my imagination run away with me, thought Danni. She squinted out to sea again to check out the fishing boat.

Then she heard the muffled braying of a distressed donkey. It sounded as though it was coming through a tunnel. Danni spun round to locate its whereabouts. It was coming from the foot of the cliffs.

At first Danni didn't notice the cave. Its gaping mouth looked like a dark shadow cast by one of the tall standing stones nearby. But then she saw it. And as she edged forward to investigate, Danni spied the front of the cattle-wagon peeping out from its darkest depths.

Suddenly, Danni's heart lurched. The dull, muffled braying echoed in her ears. And her face burned with anger.

She crept as close as she dared. Then realized that the wagon was unattended. Further along the shore, perched on a flat rock, was the driver. He sat there, smoking and staring out to sea.

Danni moved like a shadow herself, slipping from rock to rock, stone to stone, until she was at the mouth of the cave. The next minute she was inside.

Danni pressed her face against the wagon's side, trying to peer through the tiny airholes.

'Daisy! Jasper,' she whispered. Her voice hushed the pitiful braying. Eight pairs of ears pricked forwards in desperation, clinging to every word she said. Her voice had a calming effect on the donkeys.

'Don't worry. I'm here,' soothed Danni. 'And I'm not going to let anything happen to any of you.'

She reached up and tried the lever securing the end ramp. The lever turned slowly beneath her grasp. The ramp eased open 30 centimetres. Two holding rods stopped it from opening any further. Danni was just trying to work out how to remove the rods when she heard the warning sound of footsteps on the beach pebbles. The driver was coming back.

Danni shinned up the rear of the wagon and squeezed through the opening she had made.

Now she was inside with eight terrified donkeys. It was unbearably hot, stuffy, and stifling.

Danni could hardly breathe. She peered into the darkness. It was pitch black.

Instinctively Danni stretched out her arms. Her hands touched a damp woolly coat. The donkey trembled with fear. She found its neck and head. Then its furry face. She stroked it tenderly and gave it a hug.

There were seven others, including Daisy and Jasper. She found each one in turn and offered the comfort of human contact.

The donkeys were untethered inside the wagon and crowded Danni closely to huddle near. Daisy and Jasper buried their heads in her arms. And Danni wept.

Crabby Quay—Bellchurch

Jenny Lester peered up the road then checked her wristwatch anxiously. She exchanged a quick glance with Tim and Kristie.

'Danni and Shadow should be here by now!'

'Maybe she's taking it easy,' suggested Tim. But he knew that sounded really stupid. Danni and Shadow *never* took it easy.

Robert Richards aimed his camera along the cobbled road and focused his lens on the horizon. He wanted to capture the moment when Shadow's fish-cart first appeared, as it bounced over the rise.

Television cameras were in position and ready to roll. Crowds lined the quayside, waiting patiently. The only thing missing was Danni and Shadow.

Wreckers' Cove

Danni knew that she didn't have much time. She left the donkeys with a promise of her return and squeezed her way back out of the wagon, through the gap in the ramp.

Dropping from the wagon, Danni landed noisily on the shingle floor of

the cave. The sound echoed off the walls. She quickly found the rear wheels and twisted the valves off the tyres. Air hissed from the ruptures.

Next moment she was being grabbed by the arms and pulled roughly to the front of the cave.

'Where did *you* spring from?' snapped the driver angrily as he yanked Danni off her feet. He didn't seem so charming now. He sounded rough and horrible.

Then he recognized Danni. 'Why, it's the little donkey girl,' he sneered. 'You're supposed to be raising money for that stupid sanctuary of yours. Not poking your nose in where it's not wanted.'

Suddenly he heard the air escaping from the tyres. 'What's that noise?' he began. '. . . Why, you little . . .' Danni squirmed from his grasp and kicked him hard on the shin. As hard as she could. The driver let go. And Danni ran.

She was fast, but so was the driver. Danni scrambled back across the pebble beach, kicking and slipping on the stones. The man was right behind her. Gaining. Getting closer.

Danni put on a spurt and ducked out of reach as he lurched forward to grab her. She cleared the shingle ridge and headed up the lane.

Shadow's ears twitched. He looked back across his withers and saw Danni racing towards him.

'Go, Shadow. Go!' Danni yelled at the top of her lungs.

The man was almost upon her. The little black donkey pricked up his long ears and scraped a hoof on the ground.

Danni reached the cart and kicked out the brake blocks, seconds before her arms were pinned to her sides in a vice-like grip.

'S-h-a-d-o-w! Runnnn!' Danni screamed. 'Fetch help.' The little donkey didn't hesitate. He shot off like a bullet. Ears forward. Head down. He tore up the lane, alone. Shadow ran the only way he knew—mega fast. Super speed. He was a rocket, flying back along the lane to fetch help.

When he reached the junction, Shadow shied to the left and found himself on the straight run into Bellchurch.

Nothing could stop him now. Shadow flew like there was no tomorrow. He was the fastest thing on four legs.

Crabby Quay—Bellchurch

Robert, the photographer, was poised with his camera. Suddenly a cloud of dust appeared over the horizon.

Click! Whirrr! Click! Whirrr! Click! Whirrr! The camera shutter caught the precise moment that Shadow breached the rise. Hoofs flashed and sparked on the ancient cobbles as the black racing donkey burst into Bellchurch.

'It's Shadow,' yelled Tim.

'But where's Danni?' Jenny Lester squinted into the sunlight. 'I just knew it,' she said. 'Something's wrong!'

Before anyone could move or say another word, Jenny shot forward to meet the speeding donkey. Kristie rushed to help. Cameras clicked and rolled. Crowds cheered. And Crabby Quay burst into rapturous applause.

But beneath the excitement and roar of the supporters, Jenny Lester was worried.

'Danni must have found something,' said Tim. 'She would never send Shadow on alone.'

The little donkey blew a vigorous snort. He knew he was amongst friends. And now he wanted to lead them all back to his very best friend of all . . . Danni.

It only took minutes for Jenny to spring into action. She leapt into the fish-cart with Tim at her side. Then she waved to Kristie.

'Tell Robert and Martin to follow with the horsebox. And call the police,' she yelled across her shoulder, as the cart shot off at breakneck speed, out of Crabby Quay and back along the cobbled causeway.

Wreckers' Cove

La Sombra manoeuvred its way between the savage rocks. The fishing smack then beached itself, five metres from the shore. A mounting ramp dropped from the back of the boat, down into the surf. The engine died and spluttered into silence as the anchor slipped into the water.

Danni was locked inside the cattle-wagon's cab as the driver began leading the donkeys down to the shore. She banged against the windscreen. She thumped on the steering wheel and blasted the horn. But there was no one to hear her in Wreckers' Cove. No one, except the gulls. And a little black donkey, not far away.

Shadow pricked up his ears and ran as fast as he knew how. He pulled the cart and carried Jenny Lester and Tim down the lane into Wreckers' Cove. Robert Richards and Martin Green followed in the horsebox. The police were close behind.

Six donkeys had already been dragged up the ramp on to *La Sombra*. Danni was screaming against the cab's windows as Daisy and Jasper were being pulled across the pebbles towards the boat. She couldn't believe this was all happening, right before her very eyes. And she was powerless to do anything.

The con-man had won. He was getting away with his prized cargo. Danni felt totally helpless as she watched Daisy and Jasper being forced to climb the loading ramp on to the boat.

A surly looking man was helping. It was *La Sombra*'s captain. The donkeys brayed pitifully as they were finally hauled up on to the deck.

Tears stung Danni's eyes, blinding her vision as the ramp slowly began to rise out of the shallow water. It clunked into place, filling the loading gap at the rear of the boat. Then the anchor was pulled and the two men strung a canvas canopy over a framework across the deck. The canopy hid their cargo from prying eyes. Now *La Sombra* looked just like a harmless fishing smack. No one would ever guess that it was smuggling donkeys out of

England. And no one would be looking for it. Therefore no one would see it—like a shadow, *La Sombra* had almost become invisible.

The engines burst back into life. The boat was ready to leave. Danni kicked at the cab door but it was useless. She was hopelessly locked inside. She suddenly realized that she could be there for ages. The driver wasn't even bothering to come back for the wagon. It was probably stolen anyway, and brought across on the same boat, guessed Danni. Hidden beneath that same canvas canopy.

Danni felt sick with despair and slumped back in the driver's seat. But then she heard something. Even inside the confines of the cab she could hear an unmistakable sound, loud and clear. A foghorn braying— a deafening, ear splitting donkey drone. It was Shadow, calling at the top

of his lungs, bellowing like a pirate, 'Yawwwwwww!' With a mad whirring of wheels and a clattering of hoofs on the loose pebbles, Shadow and his fish-cart flew into the cove.

Within seconds, Jenny and Tim had leapt out onto the beach and were racing down to the shore.

Shadow stood on the shingle ridge and called to the other donkeys out on the boat.

The noise he made even drowned out the rattling chug of the boat's throbbing engine. No

one will ever know what Shadow actually said, but the donkeys on board heard him loud and clear. And they all responded, immediately.

Suddenly, there was mayhem on board. The donkeys went berserk. They kicked and bucked. They stamped and reared. They turned wild and tore at the canvas canopy with their teeth.

They ripped and pulled and caused such a commotion. The captain left the wheel and was shouting at his friend to control the cargo. He raised a stick to strike the donkeys. But Daisy got there first. She raised her hind legs and delivered such a tremendous kick that the captain went flying overboard into the water.

Jenny and Tim waded through the

85

surf and climbed aboard. They pulled themselves up onto the deck just as Kristie, Martin, and Robert arrived at the beach.

Jenny pushed past the man blocking her way on the deck, and struggled to reach the bridge. She killed the engine and whacked the winch lever, dropping the anchor back into the water.

The man made a grab for her, but Tim flew onto his back and knocked him off balance. Then Jasper broke loose and came to the rescue. He caught the man by the seat of his trousers and clamped his teeth shut like a vice.

'Get that thing off me,' he yelled. Then a look of terror swept across his face as the other donkeys broke free and surrounded him, braying noisily, lips rolled back showing their teeth. Ears were flat, eyes were wild.

Kristie, Martin, and Robert made it to the boat. They hit the deck and helped Tim and Jenny to calm the donkeys.

Then the sound of a police siren split the air and two officers raced across the pebbles onto

the beach. Next minute they were in the surf.
One grabbed the captain while the other hauled
himself aboard.

It was all over very quickly. Suddenly *La
Sombra* wasn't going anywhere. And the
donkeys were safe.

Jenny and Kristie calmed the donkeys.
They were all terribly over excited and in
desperate need of food and water. But,
thankfully, they were all OK. And more than
pleased to be led safely off the boat and back
onto the beach.

It didn't take long for them to discover the cattle-wagon. Danni was blasting the horn and yelling against the windscreen. She had seen everything from the cave and was cheering at the top of her voice.

Shadow ambled down onto the beach. He had stood poised with the fish-cart and watched all the donkeys being led off the boat.

Danni rushed up to Shadow and gave him a huge hug. The little donkey waggled his ears excitedly. He had saved the day.

'Right,' said Jenny. All the donkeys were safely boarded into the horsebox. They'd been fed and watered, and were feeling more comfortable now, with their feet on a bed of fresh, dry straw, and the sound of reassuring voices in their ears.

The two crooks had been taken for questioning to the police station in Bellchurch, and everything seemed to have worked out brilliantly.

'We saved the donkeys,' declared Danni triumphantly.

'But we've still got the trek to finish,' added Jenny, 'before we can take our new residents home. Do you still feel up to it?' she asked. 'I'd understand if you didn't.'

Danni grinned. Her smile said it all.

'Come on, Tim. We'll ride into Crabby Quay together.' Shadow cleared his nostrils with a loud snort as Tim leapt into the cart and settled himself next to her.

'This one's for The Sanctuary,' called Tim. Danni flicked the reins and Shadow shot forward, at rocket speed.

'See you at the Quay,' she yelled back into the wind.

Jenny and Kristie laughed as the back of the fish-cart disappeared in a cloud of flying dust towards the Quay. Shadow's hoofs barely touched the ground. He was steaming!

The Sanctuary—Whistlewind Farm— one week later

The point-to-point donkey trek had been a mind-blowing success. The television coverage had generated more donations than they could ever have imagined. And when the newspaper ran the donkey abduction story, a local sawmill offered to provide all the wood The Sanctuary needed to build its wintering barns.

It couldn't have worked out better. Jenny Lester traced all the donkeys' owners, and re-assured them that The Sanctuary *really would* provide a lifetime of loving care and devoted attention to their woolly coated friends.

The donkeys themselves stayed together in one large group. They shared the same stable block and paddock. Their terrible ordeal in the cattle-wagon somehow formed an invisible bond between them, and they refused to be separated.

Jasper and Daisy had always been close. Now they were stuck together like glue. They almost had to be prised apart with a crowbar when the farrier came to pedicure their hoofs.

Dolly, Captain, and Dixie followed the two sanctuary donkeys everywhere. Old Grey and Rosie became an instant couple, but stayed very close to the others.

Blue was the oldest donkey at The Sanctuary. The vet thought he was probably at least forty years old, which made him the grandfather of donkeys. He was very gentle and quiet and liked to sleep a lot with one eye slightly open, keeping the rest of the group in close sight. The other donkeys took turns to check on him throughout the day. They would approach the old boy and gentle rub muzzles to reassure him that he was safe.

Danni and Tim watched them for hours. It was great being at The Sanctuary. They were living with donkeys. And there was nothing quite like it in the whole world. It was brilliant.